TASKER STREET

TASKER STREET

Mark Halliday

The University of Massachusetts Press Amherst

Printed in the United States of America
Designed by Edith Kearney
Set in Minion by Keystone Typesetting, Inc.
Printed and bound by Thomson-Shore, Inc.

Library of Congress Cataloging-in-Publication Data

Halliday, Mark, 1949–
Tasker Street / Mark Halliday.
p. cm.
ISBN 0–87023–776–4 (alk. paper). — ISBN 0–87023–777–2
(pbk. : alk. paper)
I. Title.
PS3558.A386T3 1992
811′.54—dc20 91–41031 CIP

British Library Cataloguing in Publication data are available.

Some of the poems in *Tasker Street* have appeared in periodicals:

"New Wife" in *Agni*
"Fidelity" and "Joan Armatrading" in *Cimarron Review*
"My Strange New Poetry" in *Columbia*
"Seventh Avenue," "Polack Reverie," and "Reality U.S.A." in *Crazyhorse*
"The Turn" in *Denver Quarterly*
"The Truth" and "Springtime For You" in *The Gettysburg Review*
"Already in 1927" in *The Kenyon Review*
"Lionel Trilling" and "Chekhov" in *Mississippi Review*
"64 Elmgrove," "Population," and "Winchendon" in *New England Review*
"Failure" in *Southwest Review*
"Vegetable Wisdom," "Grief," and "Another Man," and "Fox Point Health Clinic, 1974" in *Virginia Quarterly Review*

The three italicized lines in "Shopping With Bob Berwick" are from Theodore Roethke's poem "A Walk in Late Summer."

Contents

TASKER STREET

THE TRUTH

The truth was there, beside the road
but you never looked straight at it. The other
two poems were there in the book you held
but you never quite read them.
A small girl in a hotel corridor,

a proof about a circle around a triangle,
a phrase including the word "reciprocal,"
a film about pornography
juxtaposed with an essay on Thoreau
plus some sense of purpose in a landscape by Watteau,
a wave crossing your mind when you sang
"Hello Goodbye" on Compo Beach—
you never got the hint.
Riding past a graveyard watching the traffic;
the truth was there, was it not, maybe
something about the tombstones being among
such lovely trees?—How the trees come
abruptly and almost theoretically right out of the ground . . .

Intersection of two memories:
your mother downtown saying "That poor creature,"
your friend at a barbecue saying "So many kinds of goodness."
"Ode to a Nightingale"—
what if you were to really read it again
instead of just examining it?
And there was a scene in *Jude the Obscure*
the color of which was dark dark green;
or possibly the meditations of a strange woman
published by some small press in California—

but maybe not in a book at all.
You want it to be in a book,

one poem or one story, or one picture, you want it
to be in one place.
Has that been your mistake? But what do you mean by
the truth?
"If I could tell you that, I wouldn't be missing it."

Your friend Laird sat in the kitchen at midnight
drinking tea. You got home from rehearsal and sat down
with a piece of carrot cake and told Laird about
the latest power struggles in the theater group.
He listened, and after a while he read aloud a paragraph
from *Howards End.* What paragraph, on what page?
"We try to make something," Laird said,
"that other people can use." "That's how you know
if you've done it," he said, "you see if
certain other people can use it." Laird said
something like that, and you answered, and
that kitchen seemed the right place to be—
but now
you're not sure what was meant.
Still

there must be a reason why
now and then you get this feeling that the truth

was right there
though you kept looking a few degrees north of it,
never saw it head-on.
You were only human.
And you did keep looking, didn't you? (Let's give
credit where credit is due.)
"That's true too."

NEVILLE CAIRNS

Though I walk with a rather strange slight limp
due to my calcium deficit which involves
various chemical failures of my body which seem linked
to some weakness of spirit—and
though my body's inadequate production of histamine
makes me quite weirdly sluggish some days
staring at the ceiling sorry for all wretched persons
stuck in this treacherous life—and
though in five years no woman has slept with me
because when they come close they see my rigid tension
which is not subject to my control not to mention
my odd limp and anyway I always queer it
by talking of my iron-spined father the Colonel
and of my rages and
                                        the lift-off from the body
which *has* come sometimes on the far side of rage

still, still when I pick up some poetry,
what I want—
I don't want to be dragged through, you know,
the rottenness of existence—the disgust
and ball-crushing disappointment—
because you see I've been there, I've done that.
So I don't need poetry that tastes like
dust in the mouth, thank you all the same.
What I want—
not that I pick up poetry so often, because
generally I'm too tired or too rattled
to concentrate properly; but
if I do pick up a poem, you know,
while my leg-bones and hips are aching and indeed
almost squeaking in their extraordinary way
and my left hand has this odd slight tremor

what I want is a glimpse, shall we say,
of marble columns in a great temple where each step taken
echoes like the step of a giant, and where
between the marble columns in a shaft of sunlight—
it's a question of some alternative, isn't it,
a question of there being something *else*—
if you ask me what it is I'll have to say
"I'm not the poet, am I" but what comes to mind
(at the risk of being jeered) is Sondra Finchley,
a girl who danced with me once in Killarney
for a minute and a half.
She'd be there (let us say) wearing a silk shirt:
Sondra Finchley but in gentleness much improved.

VEGETABLE WISDOM

You want to tell me how it seemed
the day you fell in love at the Blue Parrot
and the night in Washington Square when you felt
a weird hitherto undescribed floating absence of love
and how much it hurt that day on Waterman Street
across from Faunce House when the cars passing
were just clots of metal and the poetry books
were just wads of flattened wood because
Cathleen had walked away . . .
You want to spill those old dark beans.
They seem to choke you. They threaten to burst
with undigested meaning—

but why does it have to be me, a total stranger
who has to listen and soak it all up?
Your trust in me is a strange miscalculation;
you seem to believe I'm a future lover or brother
whose heart holds a certain space waiting to be filled
precisely by how you feel about how you felt
in Dilemma XY or Situation Q.
No, baby. You have the wrong number,
you were sold some bad information; I am someone
quite other. To me
the exact shading of how your mother in her gold bathrobe
suffered through her final months
(as perceived by you)
and how your father was brave in the silence of the kitchen
(as perceived by you)
is only distantly of interest like bright clothing
that flaps on a line behind some humble dwelling
seen from a fast bus. You see what I'm saying?
I'm a kind of receiver who can take your jewels of memory
and call them beans, beans you want to throw up.
It's a dubious metaphor but I don't really care
the way you in your bean-puffed pride feel sure

I must care—I am something *else,* you sensitive drip!
You're so pitifully pleased to address a total stranger
but that's because you have no idea how totally I am
a stranger. Will you take some advice from a stranger?
Put that poem back in your fat little filing cabinet.
And then what? Then what? Then try to be strong:
like a plant, a bush, a tree;
a tree's nobility is poemless.
My own agenda is to grow and fulfill myself
without bothering anybody else, under the stars, under the sun,
with the wind in my hair, smelling the salt sea breeze,
hearing the indecipherable songs of birds
and the alien croaking of frogs content to be frogs.
One zucchini does not ask another zucchini for praise.

GREEN CANOE

If I were sitting in a green canoe on a hot morning
having drifted gently into an odorous swamp, alone
with the speckled gross density of yellow-green slime
all around me and the sun on my head
I might then say
"It's not about books"
aloud to the plants and the muck and a swimming frog
"It's not about books"
with the sun on my head and shoulders and the world
odorous and its oeuvre oozing and green
and my saying so then might be very beautiful—

but no one would hear it—
no one would keep it—
my voice washing instantly into lost molecules in the
warm air over the swamp—
I could speak again "It's finally not
about books" but still no one hearing it
and less beautiful now,

my hand tightening cautiously on the paddle

SHOPPING WITH BOB BERWICK

We used to hit the mall those winter nights
to get away from grading quizzes ("Your work is improving,
keep at it!") and thinking of women. Shoppingtown
was big and bright and the salesgirls had legs,

hips, convexities; and chewed gum.
Slush lined the parking lot in long dirty stripes.
"We'll find the product," Bob said—to stop the mud
that kept creeping up my stairs on my boots

and right into my bedroom. Life was
a series of practical problems and nothing else:
Bob found a department called House and Yard
and there was my Coco-Mat for twenty bucks.

We drove the coarse fibrous thing to my apartment
and it sort of worked against the mud.
It was useful. Bob was useful. He had a car
and a TV; we said we cared about pro football.

Dirty snow choked the fast lanes around Syracuse
and Bob grew morose. At restaurants we spent
twice what we said we'd spend and didn't resist
apple fritters for dessert—warm

and sweet and heavy in a generous way
like a woman's breast. The similarity was
incomplete. "What a man needs," we said,
"is Raquel Welch." We laughed saying this

on the road between Shoppingtown and another mall
and Bob beeped the horn. By late winter
we weren't laughing, we bored each other,
ate out less to save money. Life was

a coarse and fibrous effort with brown exigencies;
living was what you did without Raquel Welch.
Syracuse
was where comradeship couldn't matter enough.

Beyond the ridge two wood thrush sing as one.
Being delights in being, and in time.
The evening wraps me, steady as a flame.

Late at night I ran fingertips over
poetry spines, puzzled: art and women
seemed impractically the same thing
from so many cold miles off. Three miles west

Bob watched TV. At dawn we both rose in time
to write "This reflects poor study habits"
or "Find a topic you can *care* about"
and sip coffee in our not-too-muddy kitchens.

SEVENTH AVENUE

Late Tuesday afternoon the romantic self weaves
up Seventh Avenue amid too many lookers, too many
feelers: romance hates democracy;

how can *you* be so great and golden inside
if your trunk is shouldered among other trunks
block after block, block after block—

you can't help glimpsing an otherness in others
that is not just surface: they ache,
their aches ache away north and south all Tuesday

in murmurous torsos like yours . . .
What apprehension blossoms even now in Manuel
shifting steaks at the ten-foot grill of Charley O's

beneath the towering chef's hat they make him wear?
When I was twenty I'd have written
that he was only thinking of Cadillacs and sex;

now I'm afraid he's just as worried as I am
about love vs. lesser things and the point of it all.
Manuel, stay there at the sizzling grill till midnight

and then just drink or sleep, man,
don't write poems—
do me that favor. It's loud enough already

out here on Seventh Avenue with that cat's boom box
and these three giggle girls being Madonna together
and that guy hawking wind-up titans wielding laser lances.

Who's Wordsworth for any extended period on Seventh Ave?
In this pre-dusk traffic you catch the hint
that Manuel and thou if seers at all are seers only

for seconds—now the steak, taxi, buttocks, headline
and wallet resume their charismatic claim to be what counts.
Soul on Seventh is a sometime on-off quick-flip thing . . .

What I want is a poem long as Seventh Avenue
to sprinkle gold on every oppressed minority,
every young woman's subtly female hips,
every sad and suspicious American face
and the quiddity of every mud-tracked pizza shop;
proving, block after block, stanza by stanza
that I'm not just one skinny nervous pedestrian
but the one who matters because he sees and says.
I want that. The Avenue grins and says
"You want that? How does it feel to want?"

ON THE HISTORY OF POETRY

Two black guys move along Spruce Street
in West Philadelphia. One of them carries
a bottle in a paper bag. They look healthy
but tense and tired. It's about six p.m.
What is it to them if you sit on a porch
in Tennessee writing about how we all become dust
that will sift through sunlight one day quietly?

My wife has a cold and her voice is different,
I love her sitting at the table with books
titled *Dyslexia* and *Human Memory* working
cheerfully though she doesn't feel great. She is
half-listening to "No Compassion" by the Talking Heads.
It's an amusing song and part of the history of poetry.
"We are white," I find myself thinking, "and not
terribly important." I'm thinking this because
we don't know anyone here; till a month ago
we lived in Boston and figured in
the daily lives of some twenty or thirty hearts.
There like anyone anywhere, like a famous poet or
garage mechanic in Tennessee we had our local stories
with our own mosaic of datum and sensation—
but friends made "local" seem rich, not small.
Tonight we're just a couple in an apartment,
feeling lonely and whatnot; to find us

you have to dig deep into the recent back stacks
of the infinite history of poetry, on the hundredth floor
of the newest Philadelphia wing.
Darkness falls. The black men read
a preseason report on the Eagles and
an article on desegregation of the computer industry
and soon fall asleep in their separate buildings.
What they said at dinner has already gone spinning
up sky-colored ramps to small locations in
the history of poetry. Annie and I

talk a little about our friend Peter's new poem
and go to sleep. It's a warm night.
The morning is warm and hazy.
A Korean woman in South Philadelphia
comes downstairs looking for the mail
but there isn't any. She picks up
her grandson's yellow plastic Jeep and watches
a pigeon patrolling the curb, and feels something.

—1983

LIONEL TRILLING

After one of those library hours that decompose into
a bummer, the vast bummer of the unread, I bump into
Greg and we go to the Honeydew for coffee and I say
there is some book, I mutter this several times
so Greg says what book what do you mean some book
and I say there is some one book one book I need

and he says for what, need for what, and I say
to make things take shape, to make a shape,
I can feel that there's this one book for me to read
today, not next week, not next month but what is it
so Greg says well what would it be about would it be
poetry or a novel or what and I say maybe it's by

Lionel Trilling—essays, then, Greg says
you feel a need for good literary essays. Maybe,
maybe, I'm not sure, for a minute I thought it was
a novel by Shirley Ann Grau, then I thought maybe
some book of poems with the word *Door* in the title
but then I saw, I just glimpsed a book by

Lionel Trilling—I was on my way out of the stacks
I just glimpsed the spine but something about his name
so Greg says you're getting yourself rattled, relax,
you can go back and check out Trilling this afternoon
but I say no I have to go home and besides it's as if
the chance has passed, the moment has passed

and he says you're a sick mystic. We drink more coffee
and I eat a brownie and we lapse into our ambition talk
about what we wish or don't wish we could write
and I say greatness is finding the ideas you really need
(or something) and we mention Eliot Pound Yeats Stevens Frost
as usual and feel small with our coffee

and walk out into the dizzle of traffic, the brumble of
students and cars and signs just glimpsed
and it's that ol' gray river of time, we say one thing or
another and Greg happens to mention that
the cover of his new book will be purple and I say
purple that's good, purple, that's good, it's of the heart.

CHEKHOV

He says she has lovely gray eyes
but then later the fence is gray and the sea is gray
and those are like bad things, so I wondered

Is he trying to help us or just show us
What do we finally *get* from Chekhov
in this story, do we feel that he makes us see
our lives in the bafflement of—
Well, I just got an image of this current
running under everybody's life

Go a little further with that

Wasn't sure if I was reading that in
or if it was really there
To see how effective understatement can be
and that was, that was the impression I got
But effective for what
He goes out in the garden and these shapes
rise and disappear in the mist
He doesn't know *why* he's going to sleep with her and
Chekhov doesn't—
You can't say for sure it's not love

The wet snow and the black trees and the smoky train

Like a current that runs under everybody's—
no matter what they do
Is it good? It's life. Is it good? It's life.
(the traffic on 34th Street vum vum vum)
I didn't get that much didn't get that
Like poetry because it leaves so much unsaid
Okay next time we'll do the next story
(young Nancy's brown eyes)

THE TURN

The scene was green but the sky was blue;
the sky was blue but the house was brown,
and so I thought

Just then, as that voice echoes still in one's mind,
a blue Volkswagen will turn the corner and one will see

One sparrow sprang from an icy branch
into the winter sky, and in my heart it was as if

But she did not smile, and I knew

The wind carried a smell of burning
as we crossed that field toward our old life together,
and it came to me then

And now when I study this Instamatic snapshot
I find myself aware at last

The song spills out in the September air
above the silent, scummed, enduring pond
and you think again

The song spills out through the July air above
the fecund pond just as it did you know when
and you think

Pulsing like blood the memory swells
through a pinkish haze and he understands

The experience washed over us, a dark
and salty wave, and became a shape
in our constant, secret, fabulous game; oh then,
it seemed, the world for a tiny while made sense.

ODE: THE CAPRIS

How do I feel about "There's a Moon Out Tonight"
by the Capris?
I thought you'd never ask.

Marcia Koomen lived across Cherry Lane
getting tall, taller than me in fifth grade
and smiling behind her glasses, she knew something.
The summer nights in Raleigh were thick
with something bright in the dark; you could ride
bikes under the moon and in and out of
lampshine at the corner of Wade and Dogwood,
not caring about touching a girl, or, later,
not caring much still but happy to be a boy
who could some day "have" a girl, and conscious of
a shivering beauty caught in the word *girl*

There's a girl at my side
that I adore
—the Capris knew something all together
and it called for this new verb, to adore;
something out there ahead of my bicycle in the dark;
I cared a lot about Paladin on "Have Gun—Will Travel"
but did I adore him? Scotty Koomen, years older,
got sort of pale and brittle when he went to visit
a certain girl in his class, he seemed to have trouble
breathing . . .
There's a glow in my heart
I never felt before
—not exactly in my heart yet but it was
what *would* be there if I rode just maybe deeper down
Dogwood Lane in the busy dark.

Across Dogwood lived Ann Dailey
who had freckles and an awesome kind of largeness,
not fat but big and this made my eyes feel hot and burny;
she moved slowly doing chores in her yard,

her long tanning thighs seemed sarcastic
as if she knew soon her freckled beauty must positively
carry her somehow out, out and away . . . And
Shelby Wilson one night kissed her on the lips.
I saw it happen—on the sofa in the basement—
her folks weren't home. Right on the lips!

Amazing lips are in your future, boy. That's
what the Capris were telling me; the North Carolina moon
is natural and it can find you anywhere:
you have to let the moon paint you and your bike
and the picture of Elvis in your pocket
and it shines down on Marcia's hair
and on the thought of the green eyes of Ann Dailey.
Ride and wait, wait and watch;
you laugh, you shiver in the summer-cool-dark,
you speak of the Yankees and the Pirates but
cut a side glance at Marcia's tall shape
but when she says anything serious exasperate her
yelling Little Richard's wop bop alu bop

but this dodging, dodging will end—
somewhere—
the Capris being on Marcia's side.
Baby, I never felt this way before
I guess it's because there's a moon out tonight

and once that shining starts
no amount of irony will ever quite ride the Capris out of town.
I picture a deep pool with yellow flowers drifting
on the surface. The song pours up
out of that pool.

ROOTS

How good is it to know where you came from,
what people you came from and what they believed?
My mother never spoke of her parents—
they had somehow seen her as a bad girl
and she left Canada forever.
My father occasionally spoke of his grandparents
but it never seemed as if I had to listen . . .
Michigan—

in a small Michigan town two horses clop along
the dirt street under a blue sky
and the riders in the buggy or wagon or cart
believe in Jesus Christ
and the grownups can remember England.
They must have ideas about Oliver Cromwell
and William Pitt and Napoleon
and Andrew Jackson.

But I just found myself alive
in Raleigh, North Carolina
with my Davey Crockett cap and my Fanner .50,
my mother gave me a milkshake with an egg in it
each day after first grade so I'd get strong,
because you need to be strong to do things, to live,
and you just want to live.
I learned the word "agnostic" to tell what I was,
my father's friend Jack Suberman chuckled when I said
"McCarthy is an alligator,"
soon I had ideas about Mickey Mantle and Roger Maris—
men who came from nowhere, who had always been Yankees,
who stepped from nowhere to the plate and clobbered the ball.

Then in 1964 in the ping-pong room in Connecticut
what mattered to Trey and Jon and me was the Beatles,
their every syllable: brown-haired angels,

the radiant big boys that we might become.
They were British, well, wasn't I sort of British
with a name like Halliday? It was good not to be
faintly peculiar like a Jew or a Catholic;
at the same time we were all Americans and that was good too
for freedom, freedom from old dark worries and popes and kings.
We sang "It Won't Be Long" and "Any Time At All"
in our church of albums . . .
Upstairs, Daddy was an expert on Hemingway's heroes.
He got me to read stories about Nick Adams—
you had to be brave because you would be alone
some day in the forest or in a big city.
And it was important to work hard in high school,
the quadratic theorem and molecules
and the Reign of Terror leading to Napoleon
then go to a famous college.
It was just important.
With no God or Bible
there was sometimes a funny emptiness
in the car on North Avenue

but I had the Beach Boys, I had the Byrds,
I had the Lovin' Spoonful in a world all new;
one day in twelfth grade suddenly there was *Rubber Soul*
proving forever what you needed for the right life:
romantic love, humor, brilliant freshness—
that was it!
The universe had given *Rubber Soul* into our chosen hands.

64 ELMGROVE

I was there, that was me, there I was in the gray light,
that day slipped like a raft on the Susquehanna,
like a raft on the Shenandoah, sliding a little sideways
like an old raft of worn boards on the Housatonic;

at the kitchen sink I stood seeing yellow-brown grass
matted in the back yard of 64 Elmgrove
and time passed. Jessica traveled emphatically
down the hall in her boots defying various fears;
happiness turned on its old famous wheel
till odd silence and sad little touches took its place.
There was that tangle of wet colors in the autumn yard
and then I was gone, Jessica was long gone
and my U-Haul truck trembled with fear of change.
I am not at all a Hindu, I've never been a Hindu,
I want to keep things—

what I can't lose is the feeling that things are
taken away because I haven't understood
the right way to hold them close. "If you love me,"
Jessica said, "you have to let me grow."
And I guess I did. And there was gray light
in the kitchen, on the round table there were
white coffee mugs till the whole house floated
fast down river till I stand now staring as if
through a kitchen window at yellow-brown grass
as if staring could reassemble what was tangled and then
became a runaway raft so easily as if the white mugs
and the piano and the wine-stained rug and how Jessica walked
had not been worth keeping.

POLACK REVERIE

I don't like that it's all going out the window splish splash.
I don't like that it's all going out the window whush whush.
All pouring down the chute. Out
into the glittering blank vast winter air: Shoooofff . . .
Sooooshhhh . . .
Pouring down and out—

what I think about Alfred Tennyson this morning
and what you said about Milton last night;
what I understood in Allen Grossman's office in 1980
on the subject of "preservation of the Image of the Person"—
these things
have chemically dissolved along with
how I once did justice to "Please Please Me" with Jessica.
Jessica: somebody I knew.
Gone, gonezo: gleaming gush out the window, it's a cascade—
the taxi, the airport, the letters from ephemeral hotels . . .
Maybe you want me to shape this into stanzas,
perhaps the neat In Memoriam stanza whose fourth line suggests
a returning, circling back; but the white spaces would seem
too expensive. There is this craving for
accretive synthesis of bulked declaration
which arises from realization of
loss loss loss of what we feel and think
being different people at different times, you yesterday
murmuring "That's what you say *now*"
and me last week saying "Yeah but I'm not Samuel Beckett"—
there's a wanting to not lose lose lose but
it's trying to braid a cascade. "Can't be did."
Kimbo used to say that in a funny voice in junior high.
Friends, with their funny voices—
Jessica in 1971 made up a ridiculous song about Hedda Hopper
which I don't exactly want to remember now (Jessica—
somebody I once really knew) . . .
Away, away down the chute

out into the winter light into the streaming air into
les neiges which will be *disparues bientôt.*
I could find a line in *Andromaque* about loss loss loss
which probably gave me a *frisson* in 1965 . . .
This morning after some Tennyson
I tell Annie I've been in a poetic reverie
and she, just waking up, says "A Polack reverie? About what?
About cavalry riding out to fight the German tanks?"
(We had the same teacher for Modern European History.)
Booming against us over the cold fields come
the Panzer tanks of loss, and our horses tumble;
naught may endure but Mutability—
I think I taught that Shelley poem in 1976
at Manlius Pebble Hill School. Could there be
a more obscure name for a school? Manlius Pebble Hill . . .
An eighth grader named Edward was smart and troubled
and wanted my attention, he wanted not to be
merely gushing out the window of my life in the cascade
of eighth grade. (I almost remember his drawings of magic birds.)
Edward, boy: we fade.
But in my role as wise elder I should tell you:
be strong in the saddle
when the cavalry of wishing rides forth
extending its metaphor beyond safe territory
into the cannons of hope betrayed
like Tennyson's brigade—
Edward, boy—

FAMILY

The family drove from Colorado to Pasadena
for Christmas, and Bev unwrapped two games
to give to the boys during the trip,
because she wanted the boys to be happy—
she brought out the games in a motel in Utah—
and thirty-two years later,
thirteen years after Bev's death,
Hal for some reason remembers the motel in Utah
(while making a wry point about motels, or Utah, or Christmas)
and begins to speak of that evening—
and then at the phrase "to keep the boys happy"
he suddenly has to stop and look away.

GRIEF

Grief will come very naturally to you, into your living.
It's how your life is not a movie, the way right timing
and the firm edges of drama will not body forth
your grief like a spotlit Lear at center stage;
the way it will come ten minutes or a year after
the formally obvious hour, will come
when someone important is on vacation, when someone
(you) has to get the car back from Rocky's Body Shop.
Then it will be there, the bad news, nudging
into your life like a healthy dog that feels at home
in any house, hoisting its dirty paw among
your thoughts about the breakfast or a foreign film.

FAILURE

In the failure hotel there is a corridor.
There is not only the lobby of despair; there is
a corridor, and you can move
along the gray thin carpet through shadows,
toward shadows. It's about
what you wanted to do
and why you wanted it,
and in the farther shadows it's
why you failed. This has interest;

you turn right or left and the shadows
are deeper but they are of interest.
At another corner you turn left or right.
Because you can't just stand there.
This is an old hotel with old quiet smells.
Thousands of guests now asleep somewhere else
have walked down this corridor, their fingertips
touching the wallpaper browned like obsolete documents.
They were here. They've gone—because
no one stays in a hotel forever.
You recall this fact,

and it's then that the shadows take on an intimacy:
you begin to know where you are even before
the number appears above the right door.
There's a key in your pocket;
there may be a book open on the bed.

ANOTHER MAN

In the spring night another man
is walking past my darling.
He is one inch taller than me
and he calls out softly Hey there.
She looks. In the May night
with the trees blossoming
the eyes of the unknown man
meet the eyes of my darling.
She feels a sadness of possibility
and he feels a sadness of possibility
and what they feel is altogether so natural—

the trees blossom earnestly in the May darkness,
my darling feels that everything alive
must die some day
and the man pausing on the sidewalk
near a bed of irises
feels the same truth with a quiet honest urgency
and softly he says to my own darling
Hey there.

FIDELITY

The things we could do
with certain lovely others
are weapons we keep loaded
or at least near the ammo box
in a drawer behind the socks,
there to pull out and polish occasionally
as at a party or dinner
when a smile or drifting fingertip
whispers richly of imaginable beds—
our brandishing when it's right
being a truly amorous blood-quickener,
a way of saying *It's all for you, my beauty,*
and don't you forget it.

JOAN ARMATRADING

Just reading the title of Joan Armatrading's song
"When I Get It Right" gives me a chill, a bitter
creeping of my skin, I think because that song suggests
a woman being hurt and hurt and still searching for love,
not quitting, hence somehow strong, searching
and my love might be wrong for her and she will
survive my wrong love and go away, searching
—that chills me—
she will have *experience* after me—or before me.
I'm against that!
                                I want her to just stay at home
in an old chair upholstered by her mom, reading history
and drawing pictures of farmhouses, until—until me.
Me me me! Till she meets *me.*
Let her be bored and melancholy till she meets *me* please,
not tough, not bouncing from city to city,
from condo to condo, from cool guy to guy.
Damn, why does she have to be a *person?*
I mean that's such a painful idea.

NEW WIFE

What if my new wife sees through me in 1993
on a long August day of the greenhouse effect
and realizes that in the end I choose
five times out of six
to do what might protect my ego from its wormy fears
instead of what might help her live
or help someone else live?
In the rippling wet heat of that long day
she comes to see that my real priority
emerging beyond accidents and gestures of this week
is to publish poems and stories and thus win praise
not much because of a great Belief in the Art
but because I was unbrave on the soccer field in tenth grade
and I do not forgive myself
and because Candy Wilson did not feel moved to kiss me
in 1964 nor did Barbara Cohen in 1966
and I do not forgive myself that either
and am desperately afraid of seeing myself
as a forgettable fleck of nothing;
and she sees that my Belief in Love is therefore frail
and could bend and even break if pressed against
my myth of Great Achievement.
(Is this true?
Is this true?)
(Can writing this poem make it less true?)

All this
grows apparent to her
as we unload groceries from the car and I dish out some sour remark
about the sameness of our dinners while merciless heat reflects
up from the car's hood and sweat slips
down from my scalp, scalp of balding writer in his forties.
She sees.
What then?
She leaves me

twisting in the eyeless desert wind of being only
some forgettable self-licking small-headed egotist who can't grow up?
Or
for a long moment she ponders her choice
and imagines now she can see why
my first wife allowed herself to lose me;
then
a testing of love, the shoulders and arms of love tested
by a weight more than bags of groceries
that we haul up the dim stairs.

SUMMER PERDU

Was there a white house with black shutters
just off Grove Street that in summer was
surrounded by scarlet roses?
Did you walk past it on a hot day
wearing your sky-blue teeshirt with a patch that said
"Donati's Gulf Service"
on your way to the Corral Restaurant
looking for your big brother Billy?
Was he there eating a sausage grinder?
Did he laugh at you in a way you instantly forgave?
Did Billy drive a blue Jeep whose seats felt
wonderfully high up?
And when Billy was off somewhere
did you sit on one of the Revolutionary cannons
in the park with some girl named Julie,
near the statue of some tall green man?
Was it Julie or another kid with whom
you spent a week or at least a day
saying "Wugga wugga wugga," your secret message
derived from a Tarzan movie?
Did that happen?
And do you now wish you knew *who* that green statue was of?
And do you now find those scarlet roses bedecking
one dark space in your head and softly buzzing?

BIOGRAPHY

Henrietta Wilhelmina Louisa Haag had been
born in Stuttgart, the daughter of
a modest functionary
who later apparently
settled in Kassel.
As far as she knew she had been born
in Stuttgart; in those days you just accepted
what they told you. You were dressed
in layers. Henrietta Wilhelmina Louisa
sat by a window on a morning of rain:
the cobbles of Stuttgart must have had
a cold gleam; as she stepped uncertainly
across a wooden threshold she touched
her hair, which was partly brown.
Against the smoothness of a pewter mug
she briefly rubbed her cheek. Downstairs
her mother corrected a vendor of wares.
There was in Stuttgart this life,
then other life in Kassel; for reasons
which are obscure she was
deeply unhappy in her parents' home.
Kassel in those days was a place of long hours;
flickering lamps, sausages, corporeal churches and towers.
The Fulda ran gray and blue.
Deeply, in those days, was deep enough
that some waters never got fathomed.

SAX'S AND SELVES

I saw you going into Sax's Steak Sandwiches
but what were you thinking?
It was a hot day, the downtown traffic
smashed itself right thru, right thru.
People wore their primary colors and
touched the doors and parking meters
and bottles and quarters and steering wheels
and the hold-on bars in bouncing busses
with tough hands, tools made of tough skin.
The sun was some ten degrees hotter than
anybody expected, this being not yet summer,
people folded their jackets and went to deal.
You must have been dealing too,
but what were you dealing with?
You came out of Sax's Steak Sandwiches
with a large Coke to go,
straw stuck thru plastic lid,
but what were you contemplating?
There was sweat in all armpits,
three ten-year-old boys had a hardball,
one of them shouted "Up your ass"
and laughed. Fifteen blocks away
an enormous insurance building glittered
with its violent impregnability in the hot sky.
It was real, as real as the hot yellow gas truck,
which was as real as the spice in Sax's chili,
and so were you no doubt but

what was your real point?
I mean what did you add up to?

You caught the Dudley bus
and sat next to a blind young man
whose fingers flickered every minute or so
in something like a diffident farewell to
someone important who might not return

for a long time. Staring
at the fingernails of the rider across from you,
you tapped your foot to a song called "Staying Alive"
from a black girl's huge radio—
and you may even have hummed along
while sucking ice from your tall cup—
however, the song's meaning for you
is not apparent;

and I don't know
why you got off where you did,
chucking your drained cup in a dumpster,
rolling up your sleeves as you passed the Purity Supreme . . .
I know exactly *where* you got off
and how hot the air was

but damn you! What were you *thinking?*
I've tried, I've tried to figure it
but it comes out different each time and
I can't be bothered—really,
if you have some hang-up about Being Mysterious
it's not my problem. So unless
you're willing to give me a clue—
just the general area, the basic subject,
something to get started is all,
you don't have to fork over your whole self—
but if it's just going to be trivia,
your shoes, your Coke, your moving lips,
then forget it—I'm serious—
just forget the whole thing.

COUPLES

All the young couples in their compact cars.
He's funny and she's sensible.
The car is going to need some transmission work
soon, but they'll get by all right—
Aunt Louise slips them a hundred dollars
every chance she gets and besides,
both of them working—
Susan does day-care part-time
and Jim finally got full-time work
at Design Futures Associates
after those tough nine months as an apprentice.
Or he's in law school
doing amazingly well, he acts so casual
but really he's always pounding the books,
and Susan works full-time
for a markets research firm, she's
amazingly sharp about consumer trends
and what between her salary and Aunt Louise
Jim can afford to really concentrate on
his studies. Or he's a journalist
and so is she, and they keep very up
on the news especially state politics.
Plus she does an amazing veal marsala
and he jogs two miles five mornings a week—
and in June they'll be off to Italy again,
or Mexico; Susan's photographs are
really tasteful, not touristy, she always
reads up on the culture before their trip.
Jim slips in a wacky shot every once in a while
and everybody laughs, that's old Jim.
They use a pocket calculator at Star Market.
The car is neat and perky.
It's going to need a new battery next week
but Susan knows where there's a Sale.
They'll get by all right. They have

every one of Linda Ronstadt's albums, and
they're amazingly happy together,
Jim calls her "little bird" when they're alone
and Sue calls him Jiminy Cricket
when the sun is out and their compact car is
moving neatly thru light traffic—
they're doing fine, on the whole,
despite certain fantasies of infidelity
and furtive fears of entrapment—
there's a baby on the horizon maybe three years ahead
and they're doing fine, really, and
this is very important,
it's all very important—
but—

NOT AS IMPORTANT AS US—
not as important as me and my partner.
We drive around in our perky green Datsun
and we see the other couples on the road
and we think: Fine, go to it,
get what you can, you all have your rights . . .
But we know they don't matter the way
we matter.

Wendy's brother once was watching us
clean the summer cottage
and he said: "You two are a hot item."
That was great, and we've always remembered
that phrase—and it's true,
when we get going, we *are* a hot item.

Wendy will be up to twelve thousand next year
at her counseling job, and I'll be completing
my dissertation—after that,
we're not sure, though Wendy has
a thing about Oregon.

God, you should see Wendy's pottery
from last summer, some of her glazes
are really original (it's not just me who says so),
she has a definite talent
and the truth is
her talent matters
a great deal more
than any talent *your* partner has
or claims to have.
That's just
how it is—I can feel it.
We are key.
We are the center of what's happening

and you and your partner are somewhere
out on the periphery.
I know you think your boyfriend is
more handsome than me
or more sexy maybe, or more mature-looking;
I know you think your girlfriend
dresses better than my Maggie
or cooks better with a wok
and hits a real serve in tennis
instead of just a blooper . . .
But all that stuff is just details!
How can I explain this sufficiently—
can't you see that any achievements by you two are
beside the point?

Okay I know what you're thinking now:
that Maggie and I are just like all the rest,
no perspective on ourselves,
every couple at the center of
its own phony universe—
but you don't seem to grasp

how Maggie and I are
unique—
that is, *incomparable:*

I'm talking about an absolute here,
it's the kind of thing you have to believe in
before you'll ever understand it:
me and Maggie,
and our old red Volvo sedan;
and the idea of the future baby
with Maggie's eyes and my curly hair . . .

Other couples can go ahead and exist,
but I don't want to think about them anymore—
I need to concentrate

on our good old red Volvo,
and good old Maggie's eyes,
my curly hair,
and Aunt Harriet's pies . . .

Everything else can go away!
Please, go away.

POPULATION

Isn't it nice that everyone has a grocery list
except the very poor you hear about occasionally
we all have a grocery list on the refrigerator door;
at any given time there are thirty million lists in America
that say BREAD. Isn't it nice
not to be alone in this. Sometimes
you visit someone's house for the first time
and you spot the list taped up on a kitchen cabinet
and you think Yes, we're all in this together.
TOILET PAPER. No getting around it.
Nice to think of us all
unwrapping the new rolls at once,
forty thousand of us at any given moment.

Orgasm, of course, being the most vivid example: imagine
an electrified map wired to every American bed:
those little lights popping
on both sides of the Great Divide,
popping to beat the band. But
we never beat the band: within an hour or day
we're horny again, or hungry, or burdened with waste.
But isn't it nice not to be alone in
any of it; nice to be not noticeably responsible,
acquitted eternally in the rituals of the tribe:
it's only human! It's only human and that's not much.

So, aren't you glad we have such advanced farm machinery,
futuristic fertilizers, half a billion chickens
almost ready to die. Here come the loaves of bread for us
thup thup thup thup for all of us thup thup thup
except maybe the very poor
thup thup
and man all the cattle we can fatten up man,
there's no stopping our steaks. And that's why
we can make babies galore, baby:

let's get on with it. Climb aboard.
Let's be affirmative here, let's be pro-life for God's sake
how can life be wrong?
People *need* people and the happiest people are
surrounded with friendly flesh.
If you have ten kids they'll be so sweet—
ten really sweet kids! Have twelve!
What if there were 48 pro baseball teams,
you could see a damn lot more games!

And in this fashion we get away
from tragedy. Because tragedy comes when someone
gets too special. Whereas,

if forty thousand kitchen counters
on any given Sunday night
have notes on them that say
I CAN'T TAKE IT ANY MORE
I'M GONE, DON'T TRY TO FIND ME
you can feel how *your* note is
no big thing in America,
so, no *horrible* heartbreak,
it's more like a TV episode,
you've seen this whole plot lots of times
and everybody gets by—
you feel better already—
everybody gets by
and it's nice. It's a people thing.
You've got to admit it's nice.

REALITY U.S.A.

I feel I should go to Norfolk Virginia and drink
gin with sailors on leave from the *Alabama,* talking
baseball and Polaris missiles and Steve Martin movies,
another gin with lime juice, then Balto, Balto,
hitch-hike in and out of Baltimore for days
back and forth for days in a row discussing the jobs
of whoever gives me rides, salesmen, shippers,
small-time dispatchers of the much that can be
dispatched. For the ACTUALITY of it!

Books dominate my head. I read in them, I read at them,
I'm well into my thirties. What about real life?
The woman in the light-blue skirt
on the cigarette billboard has such big thighs!
What is it about thighs? Smooth and weighty,
weighty and smooth: you can tell there's really
something *there.* And to think that
the woman must really exist, it's a photo after all
not a painting, she is somewhere in America—
and to think that some guy gets to lie down
on her and her thighs . . . She's a model,
she probably lives in New York, New York baffles me
I know I could never find her there—but
listen, her sister lives in Baltimore,
hanging out sheets to dry from the balcony
of a light-blue house, lifting her arms—
reality. Along with

her dimly dangerous ex-husband, her speed pills,
his clumsy minor embezzlement of funds from
Pabst Auto Supply, and what else?
The boxing matches he goes to, and the stock-car races
and—maybe I should go to Indianapolis?
But I feel sure I'd be bored in Indianapolis
despite the smoky reality of Indianapolis.

But it's this idea of American experience how I don't
have it, how I ought to know the way things are really
and not just from Hemingway or Dreiser, John O'Hara or
James T. Farrell
or, say, Raymond Carver or Bruce Springsteen
but directly: first-hand: hands-on learning.
What if I were to take a Greyhound to Memphis,
quit shaving, learn to drink whiskey straight,
lift some weights (maybe I should do the weights before I go)
and get a tattoo on one bicep saying KISS OFF
and meet a guy named Eddie who chain-smokes
and rob a record store with Eddie! Yes,
we smash the glass at 3 a.m. on Davis Avenue in Memphis
and grab 300 albums and 600 compact discs
pile them into Eddie's red pickup and bingo, we're gone
in five minutes. Next day we paint the pickup yellow
and change the plates, no sweat. Eddie knows,
he knows stuff, he knows how to fence the loot
and he says next we hit a certain TV store,
he slugs my shoulder laughing, I get my piece of cash
but really it's not the cash I care about,
it's the being *involved.*
                                        Eddie thinks that's weird,
he says "You're weird, man"
and starts to act mistrustful so I leave town.
Kansas City here I come.

No, skip Kansas City, I want to save Kansas City.
Just in case.
—In case what? What am I talking about?
How many lives does a person get,
one, right? And me,
                                     I love my life with books!—
Of course it's not *just* books, I've got bills

and friends and milkshakes, the supermarket, laundromat
oh shit but still I keep feeling this thing about
reality—

the world is so loaded: a green beer bottle is chucked
half-full from a speeding Ford Mercury and that beer sloshes
exactly like this loaded world—what?
Forget the world, just take America,
sure there's the same hamburgers everywhere
and gasoline fumes but among the fumes and burgers
there's *de*tail, tons of it, you can smell it.
There are variations . . . All the stuff
Whitman claimed he saw, there's the really *seeing* that stuff!
There's—
I don't know—there's a waitress in an Arby's Roast Beef
and her name is either Donna or Nadine,
you buy the Special on the right day and you get
a free Batman 10-ounce glass, she makes a joke about it,
you say "What time do you get off work" (only this time
it's really happening) and that night Donna
or Nadine does for you what you thought they only did
in fiction . . . That's right. Next morning
her bottom in the light from the window looks so pearly
it's like home, just glad to be home.
It's April, all cool and sunny,
and across the street from Arby's there is
a ten-year-old black boy wearing red hightops
and we talk about the Braves (this is in Georgia, now,
and the asphalt glistens) and the kid says
something beautiful that I'll never forget.
Good. So then, the kid's uncle sells me some cocaine
or teaches me how to aim a pistol
or takes me for a ride in his helicopter—
there must be a few black men who own helicopters?
Up we go roaring over Georgia!

The roofs and poles and roofs
the components,
the components!
Ohhh . . . Already they’ve worn me out.

THE ZOO'S LIBRARIAN

You're flying to Boston?
I am too. But I'm going on, to Bangor.
I've never been to Maine, and I'm very excited.

I didn't know what to expect,
which is why I've brought all this luggage,
though I'm only going for a weekend,
as far as I know.
I'm wearing my long underwear, because I understand
it's even colder there than it has been here, all winter.
. . . The man I'm visiting leads a very "outdoorsy"
sort of life. He works at two Indian reservations *and*
a synagogue, in addition to practicing law.
Like me, he is a recent convert to Judaism—
and for the same reason—
his interest in a caring community.

That is something for which I have turned to Judaism—
the religion which has gradually *seized* me, I believe,
since I was thirteen.
I have a strong feeling for the discipline of faith.
I was raised in the Anglican church, and discipline
has always rested lightly on my shoulders.

Yes, I did live in Philadelphia,
and in a lovely, expensive house.
I moved there from Canada
with the man I married.
. . . I shall be happy to turn my back
on Philadelphia. I've experienced so much
degradation in this area.
There is a great deal of vandalism;
among the young people, you know, it's sheer bedlam!
In Philadelphia, there is just glass glass glass.
And in the suburb where I live now,
glass glass glass. They take it—

it's small pieces so I think it must be from windows, not bottles—
and they strew it along the Nature Walks.
. . . Yes, it's sick. It must be.
Why else would they *do* it?

One evening when I was taking care of Mr. Ashmead's dog,
it was barking, and I went to check; and at that time
the Gimbels warehouse stood over there, just beyond the railroad,
and there were two of these patrol dogs, you know,
that are absolutely *trained* to be vicious.
So I went to check on all the barking, and suddenly
along came two Gimbels guards and they
turned their revolvers on me!
They had no rational reason to do so,
I think they must have seen too many cowboy movies.
It's against the law, you know,
to turn your gun on someone like that—
but the police backed them up.
I never got any satisfaction.
That's when I decided
to get out of Philadelphia, and I moved to the suburbs.

. . .That was when I left my house.
It was a house I had paid for, but
my former husband took it away from me.
I don't know how he justifies that to himself.

Quakers are terribly egotistical people.
Oh yes, terribly egotistical. Mind you,
I believe they were right to support the North Koreans
in the war. I mean, the North Vietnamese.
Some people would not agree, but I feel America had no right
to be there in the first place.
And it is the children *there* who are affected by Agent Orange
that I really feel for. I feel for the Americans who were *doing* it,
as well, but they *chose* to do it, whereas

the children in Vietnam are
purely victims.

. . . I like dogs very much, and
animals in general. I was the Zoo's librarian for several years,
and I flew to Chicago for a convention of zoo people.
That was the last time I flew.
  Of course in Chicago too there is danger—
there are a lot of knifings.
One day I was at the doctor's here in Philadelphia
(about a problem you don't want to hear about)
and the doctor came out to speak to a little black woman
and he said, "Your husband is on the operating table,
he has been knifed."—And she hissed at him,
and she said "You shouldn't have said it!"
So I think perhaps she was the one who had done it.
And judging from the way she hissed at him, I suppose
she expected to be exonerated.

  You're sleepy.
Maybe you weren't meant to be alert this morning;
maybe you were meant to rest.
. . . I do believe in a grand design.
I believe in free will,
but I also believe there are signs everywhere,
if we will only look. One day I was out in the garden,
this was November, and I said to myself,
"I must move to British Columbia."
(It was a rather difficult period of my life.) But then
I thought, "Well, I haven't seen Maine."
And the next day a letter came
from this man in Maine.
. . . So, I could be heading for
simply a very interesting weekend,
or, I could be heading for

the start of a new life.
                    And I think that would be a good thing.

  Be careful with coffee, you know,
because it can disturb your stomach.
I had a permanent yesterday, and the man
was a true sadist—
he kept *jerking* and *pulling*
and I felt as if my scalp would come right off.
Well, after that my stomach was in such contortions!
—At the present I am exceedingly poor;
my former husband paid for my ticket,
else I wouldn't have been able to fly;
and I've been out of milk for two weeks.
But I thought "I *must* get some"
because milk always has a soothing effect on my stomach.
I mention it to you
in case you should ever need the soothing.

FOX POINT HEALTH CLINIC, 1974

In the waiting room this black woman maybe fifty sits down
right beside me. Whiskey breath; pocked face.
She looks over my shoulder at my notebook
where I've been writing about Bjorn Borg in a poem
whose point is that I should never cease
striving in life.
"That's beautiful."
A minute later: "I don't see too good."
A minute later: "I think I'm dying."
So I have to really look at her.
The Portuguese women waiting for the doctor don't seem to notice,
they murmur placidly.
My woman's eyes are round and dark.
I say "I certainly hope not."
She says "I'm all gone inside. Nothing but bones and ribs.
I've got three children.
My older son lives in Gardenia California.
My other son I don't know.
My daughter she'll be eighteen she goes to St. Patrick's."
Her eyes ask me to figure out what all this adds up to—
as if it's a technical puzzle and I'm the expert.
I nod, and look down.
She leans on me. "Every night I pray to God."
She clutches my hand and keeps it. "I'm gonna
tell you something. Love is beautiful."
I nod. "Black is beautiful too" she says.
I nod. She says "I'm not black, I'm only teasing brown."
I make my eyes look into her eyes—best I can do;
if she's teasing it's a dark shade of teasing.

"I won't bug you anymore." She rises slowly
and soberly walks out. The Portuguese women shake their heads
as if they've seen my black woman do all this before.
I have a sore throat, I wish they would vanish, simply

vanish. But they don't; and gradually I work back toward Bjorn Borg whose clarity and dedication have seemed so fine, so pure, so white.

BACK STREET GUY

You stood in the littered one-way back street
till Anton came in his rusty car jammed with boxes
left over from whatever Anton was selling last summer.
Your long thick dirty black hair swung forward
video-perfect for a second as you ducked
to climb into the back seat. Chubby stoned Ray
with his Death Master comics was in the front seat
moaning the refrain of a Doors song in that voice
that colored all the south side of town.
Corrine said Ray was really musical but that was Corrine
trying to be Christian. You hunched in Anton's back seat
with your hands on your bare knees that knobbed out
from the rips in your black jeans. "Pizza" you said
but Anton didn't reply. He was trying to tune in
a country song on the radio. Ray kept moaning
the Doors lyric out his window into the dampness
of almost dusk in the dead-level city of
people not strange enough. The dampness
and the usual smell from Enolux Corp.
made you tell Ray to roll up his window.
"Suck my sword" said Ray. Anton glanced both ways
and roared through a red light. You sank back
against damp crumpled cardboard and just watched
the hundreds and hundreds of two-story houses
bricked together on every street:
downstairs eat, upstairs shit and sleep.
People on the sidewalks, moron girls in Spandex
who don't think they'll be pregnant in two years,
old plugs proud of their right to sit on porches till death,
some middle-aged dude (me) carrying his little kid
and a blue inflated Cubs bat, planning how to finance
college for this kid so he can live off the sweat of morons.
No space in this town for any big thing, big deal big story
big life, brain, heart, change—"change"

was a hot word on the evening news while you ate
a bag of barbecue chips: crappy edgy stomach feel
but no shopper could seriously expect any different.
Anton thinks this is Indianapolis, if he beats a red light
that's like a big win for his team.
He knows this bar on the north side where you can score
some weird shit very cheap. First the drug, then pizza;
later maybe Corrine.

WINCHENDON

The bus rocks gently into some town
at 5 p.m. I sort of look at the houses and stores
the way you do from a bus just passing through;
happen to notice
                    a paperboy and his pal
in small-town America
on a forgettable side street back of the hardware store
down from the brick Methodist church—
the friend wobbling his bicycle to go slow,
the paperboy fiddling with the red strap on his sack of
evening news . . .

What evening news could there be? In Winchendon . . .
The bus thrums and I'm so okay on it.
The bus thrums and I'm thinking Winesburg, Ohio,
while in Winchendon the paperboy and friend are
already way out of sight,
                              discussing a girl named
Mary Jane,
daughter of Ned of Ned's Used Cars and Parts,
how she says one thing and means the other;
the paperboy thinking of her hair as beauty itself,
conscious that he can't explain this logically.

Up by Ned's, near where some twenty Holsteins
graze stolidly all facing away from the highway,
there's a sign BLIND PERSON
                                  and I think "That's me"
and the bus thrums
into gathering dusk
and I ride thinking "gathering dusk"
away from all that other life I meant to think of
in Winchendon:
methods of local survivors—
who's making peanut waffles for dinner,

who's playing Patience over the oil-rag wilderness of the garage,
who's singing "Hit the Road, Jack"
and who's walking fast out to the darkening Common
in the hope of some personal and effective encounter.

SPRINGTIME FOR YOU

You had an experience. It was the night
you and Zahra saw "Divorce Italian Style"
at Cinematheque, you both sipped lemonade,
Zahra's eyes were dark with her thinking about
her father. I can tell you remember it.
Judy sat in the dappled shade of the mimosas
and myrtles watching you play tennis and laughed
like music when you tripped over your racquet;
it was the morning after the call came from Kentucky.
Later her arm brushed against your arm in sunlight
and Jim Friedman drove you back to campus.
I'm sure it meant something to you the way
the car was blue and *Tonio Kröger* lay on the floor.
A cooling wind came off the nearest mountain
and what you felt was not romantic love but
something more interesting. That's what you thought.
Jim talked about Churchill and Roosevelt
while you studied photographs by somebody,
not Walker Evans but a woman, those wooden
walls, and faces, those textures of seriousness
(as you said to yourself). It was that night.
When Tommy's father played a record by Peggy Lee,
of all people, you said something that was just right.
Springtime; and you are the one who was there.

ALREADY IN 1927

Summer night in quiet level suburban streets,
lights still on in two out of three houses,
five small green lights edge the driveway
of a brick house two doors down, cold lights
in the warm dark air . . . Hundreds of lives
within three blocks—persons who look away—
and this is only one modest suburb
in North Carolina or Connecticut. Too many:
persons who are looking away. From you.

But what about 1927? Then too
lamps burned in thousands of windows
within a few miles, and were seen
through the thick of summer night meaning
lives, averted, oblivious, unreachable;
a boy and a girl said goodnight at the door

and from her window she watched him walk away
into the ripe darkness of June 1927. She felt
his steps leading to a city job and other girls,
girls with expensive hats. She felt
so small, lost and so small . . .
She sat on her bed for twenty minutes—
then she tied a paisley kerchief in her hair
and washed her face and read a novel by Hardy
and grew up and married a partly good man.
She survived the infinity of 1927:

since already in 1927 the problem was
present with all ingredients, the steps fading,
lamplight cold in the warm air on this block
and the next block . . . So
it's an old condition. The liquid darkness
and voices from the far side of the playground,
newspaper on the davenport filled

with unromantic activity, what Coolidge said
about aid to farmers; already in 1927

you had to pass through squares of darkness
and small circles of yellow light alone.
My father, for instance, was thirteen:
he shut the back door and climbed the creaky stairs,
making plans.

GRAY CHECKED SCARF

David Porter has said that for Dickinson
death is the summoner of style.
And I think of you placing your gray checked scarf
around your neck on a day in December.
Your hair, like hair that Yeats might have ached to touch,
falls across the scarf and upon the shoulders of
your black coat; we move toward the door;

the street opens upon my gaze like a new feature film
with sober intentions and I stand for a second
awed by the task of appreciation—
your hands—your eyes. There is the banquet
of what we do have while knowing it can vanish
and there is the cold banquet of what we once had
or conceivably could have had—
at both tables we gaze into the lamplit wine
and want to say something true but
not only true, something also lovely
in a respectful and charismatic sadness.
Here is the car, my dear, your gray Mazda,
and here we are in the middle of something,

unreligious, distracted, but lightly touching
each other's knees from time to time during the ride
for the sake of what has been luminous and is not gone.

NICHOLAS IN THE PARK

And they flew away, Nicholas.
But the birds will come back.

My son in the park thinks life is interesting.
He is six months old. He doesn't know
that his great-aunt Dorothy is in the hospital
breathing with difficulty, frightened of the end,
frightened by the idea of leaving
something undone, something not taken care of.
She lies in the stiff bed waiting;
faint traffic noises come from the shaded window;
there were magazines she meant to read,
there were certain old photographs to be sent
to her nephew Jimmy in Michigan;
there are three old friends with whom she hasn't spoken
in the real way, the gentle serious way,
the tone she has always been hungry for.
Stoicism has not come easily to Dorothy
though she has achieved some of it,
and now its rewards seem questionable.
She smoothes the sheet lightly with her fingertips.
Her blue eyes are deep in the mystery
of what it is to depart.
Now Nicholas, blinking his blue eyes
at the quick changes around us in the park
wonders what it is when over our heads
the rush of wings is too fast to interpret.

See Nicholas, the birds all flew away.
But they will come back.

—1988

MY STRANGE NEW POETRY

In my strange new poetry the lines will be black
and long. They will be dense with not ordinary life
but the wiry vitalism of a guy in a Pirates cap
heaving a pink rubber ball against the side of a drugstore
at midnight. There will be sentences but not
only, not always, not just properly, some stray dog
will skitter through the torn fence beside the polluted river
to half bark half growl at kids in a metal dinghy.
"Gimme the worms, Jody. Gimme those worms!"
You, you won't quite know what you think—
you won't nod your old professional approval
but like if a tall stranger in tight jeans
suddenly in the kitchen at a party touched your neck
and kissed you hard or said "You stupid bastard"
you'll step back and a minute later still feel hot
and not forget the damn poem with its nettles.
You'll sway in it like trying to move through
a rocking Amtrak express halfway to the cooked city
with both your hands out and balance turned into
mostly raw luck plus nerve—it won't be
allegorical for you, no way, it grins
and calls you Big Shot and you narrow your eyes
like a Cherokee hearing the wrong footsteps.
Gimme those worms, Jody. The back lot of
the Ramblin' Root Beer distributor has for some reason
two goats in it and in my new black lines
they too get expressed. It's a thickness
and a dark kind of living in the words
in my strange new poetry that soon I put
right on paper, next week or sooner than that.

Two years hence. When I'm ready.
After one more set of poems
about my beautiful confusion.
After I've read *Anna Karenina*
and *Don Quixote*
and the first volume at least of Proust
and one big novel by Thomas Mann—
say three years. Three years hence:

after I've written an essay about the word "enough"
and after I've done something so delectable
weaving together phrases from Henry James and Bob Dylan
and after I've written an amazing meditation on Luis Buñuel
and after I've spent a month in Frankfort, Michigan
being very real and thoughtful and full of perspective
and fresh cherry pie
then—
then—

in four years at the most—
I see it there ahead of me casting a silver shadow
back upon me now, bathing me in its promise,
validating the self that will arrive at it
in four years or less (maybe just two years?) . . .
Glimpsing it there is sometimes like already living it
almost and feeling justifiably proud.
Water pollution and toxic waste and air pollution;
the poverty of black people in my city;
the nuclear arms industry; in my moral life these things
are not just TV, they push my poems to the edge of my desk,
they push Henry James into a sweet corner,
they pull me to meetings and rallies and marches
and meetings and rallies and marches.
There I am in a raincoat on the steps of City Hall
disappointed by the turnout but speaking firmly

into the local news microphone about the issue,
the grim issue.
When I'm ready.
Four years from today!
Silver shadow

TASKER STREET

1

Johnny! Johnny?
Johnny! Ask Butchie
has he got any Super-Glue.

> The street is damp in pockets
> from rain two days ago but hot now.
> Alcoholics on the corner contend with gravity.
> Trash bits beside tires.
> In sleeveless shirts stupid boys.

Didn't I give you chewing gum Tuesdee?
Yah you dumb-ass.

> It's the sidling of reality
> forward so slowly in the sun
> past Lucky's Hoagies, not saying what for.

2

Now I have a son;
can't die young.
Can't even groove on grimness as before.

Buy the miniature basketball hoop,
write the paragraph,
catch the bus,

meet his eyes,

make a meaning shape up.

This volume is the seventeenth recipient
of the Juniper Prize
presented annually by the
University of Massachusetts Press
for a volume of original poetry.
The prize is named in honor of
Robert Francis (1901–87),
who lived for many years at
Fort Juniper, Amherst, Massachusetts